May you have power with all God's people to understand Christ's love. May you know how wide and long and high and deep it is. And may you know his love, even though it can't be known completely. Then you will be filled with everything God has for you.

Ephesians 3:18-19

Who Made God?

AND OTHER THINGS WE WONDER ABOUT

WRITTEN BY
Larry Libby

ILLUSTRATED BY
Corbert Gauthier

zonderkidz

zonderkidz
The children's group
of Zondervan

www.zonderkidz.com

Requests for information should be addressed to:
Grand Rapids, Michigan 49530

ISBN-10: 0-310-70280-1
ISBN-13: 978-0-310-70280-1

Larry Libby is represented by Alive Communications, Colorado Springs, CO

Editors: Etta Wilson, Gwen Ellis
Art Direction: Jody Langley

Printed in China
07 08 09 /CTC/ 12 11 10

For my almost-grown children,
Matt & Melissa.
Thanks for being such an encouragement
to your Dad and Mom.

Larry Libby

To Sherrie Schroeder and the staff at Most Holy Trinity
School. Your lives of faith and dedication to your
profession have enriched our children's lives in ways
impossible to measure. Thank you.

Corbert Gauthier

God Is Awesome!

Imagine you make up a word that no one in the whole wide world has ever said or even thought. One day you write your word on a piece of paper, and a pesky little neighbor kid picks up the paper, learns your word, and starts blabbing it all over the place. Before long, everyone starts using it. Your word wouldn't be so special anymore, would it? That's a little like how I feel when I say, "God is awesome."

"Awesome" used to be a strong word, but it doesn't mean anything special anymore. One person says, "I had an awesome hamburger for lunch." Another says, "I wore my awesome sneakers to school."

But "awesome" is still a special word when we use it to describe God. It means "full of awe." It's the feeling we get when we see something or someone bigger, brighter, greater, deeper, higher, stronger, or finer than anything or anyone we've ever seen before. The Bible says that God is "the great, mighty and awesome God" (Nehemiah 9:32 NIV).

We have many questions about God. It's good to ask questions. So let's ask some questions and see what we can learn about him.

If God Made Everything, Then Who Made God?

The answer is that no one made God. God, you see, wasn't "made." Everything else had a beginning, including you, but it was different for God. He didn't begin. He always has been. And always will be. Now you probably have even more questions swirling around in your head.

Imagine this. Early one morning, you open your eyes and you can smell pancakes and bacon sizzling in the kitchen. The first thing you notice is your mom sitting on your bed and looking down at you with love in her eyes.

"How long have you been sitting here?" you ask. "How did you know when I was going to wake up?"

You could go on asking her questions and more questions. Or you could just forget the questions, give her a big hug, and tumble out of bed to get a steaming plate of pancakes and maple syrup.

You could go on asking questions and more questions about God too. But finally you have to say, "It's all right if I don't understand everything about him." God just wants us to believe him, love him, obey him, and enjoy him, even if we don't have all the answers. He wants us to open our eyes every morning with thanks and gladness that a big, powerful God loves us very much.

God will be with us every morning, every night, and always.

What Does God Look Like?

When I was very little and my family would go to church, my parents would take me to the nursery, kiss me, and hand me to Mrs. Eickmeyer. Then they would tell me to learn all I could about *God*.

I liked Mrs. Eickmeyer very much. She had a big, wooden box full of toys. She told me stories about Jesus and gave me graham crackers. We had a great time. The only problem was, for years after that, I always thought that God looked like her. How was I supposed to know that Mrs. Eickmeyer wasn't God ?

Truth is, God the Father is invisible. He is a spirit. So God sent us Jesus, his Son—so we would know what he is like. And Jesus is all anyone needed to learn about God. The more we know and love Jesus, the more we know and love God.

Want to know something else? The more you and I love and obey Jesus, the more we begin to look like him! And the more we begin to be like God. I'm not kidding. I think that's the way it was with Mrs. Eickmeyer. Maybe God didn't look very much like her, but to me, she looked a lot like God.

How Can There Be a God So Big?

The more we think about how BIG God is, the more our poor heads feel dizzy. How can anyone be so great, so strong, so wise?

It took a big God to make the big oceans, big mountains, big rivers, and big heat-shimmery deserts. It took a big God to make so many stars that we can't count them.

It took a big, wise God to make all of the tiny things too. Things like perfect snowflakes with no two alike. Flowers so small you have to lie on your stomach to look at them. Shiny fish that play tag in the oceans and all the beautiful shells on the beach.

There are lots of things we don't understand about God. That's all right. We can still praise him for what we do understand. That's what the prophet Jeremiah did. He wrote: "Lord and King, you have reached out your great and powerful arm. You have made the heavens and the earth. Nothing is too hard for you" (Jeremiah 32:17).

Praise God right now. He's not too big to bend down and listen to every word!

Does God Think about Me Much?

One afternoon, Nathanael was resting under a fig tree. Nathanael's friend Philip came hurrying down the road. When he saw Nathanael, he came over to him. Philip was excited and started talking right away.

"We have found the One that Moses wrote about," he said. "His name is Jesus! Come and see." So Nathanael got up and followed Philip.

When Jesus saw Nathanael coming, he said, "He is a true Israelite. There is nothing false in him."

"How do you know *me*?" Nathanael asked.

Jesus answered, "I saw you while you were still under the fig tree."

Nathanael was excited! He knew Jesus had been thinking about him as he sat under that tree!

God thinks about YOU too. He keeps his eye on you all day and all night long. He sees when you laugh or when tears fall from your eyes. When you think about him, he is already thinking about you.

And every time you say a prayer to God, he will always say, "How good to hear your voice! I'm so glad you thought about me, because I was just thinking about you."

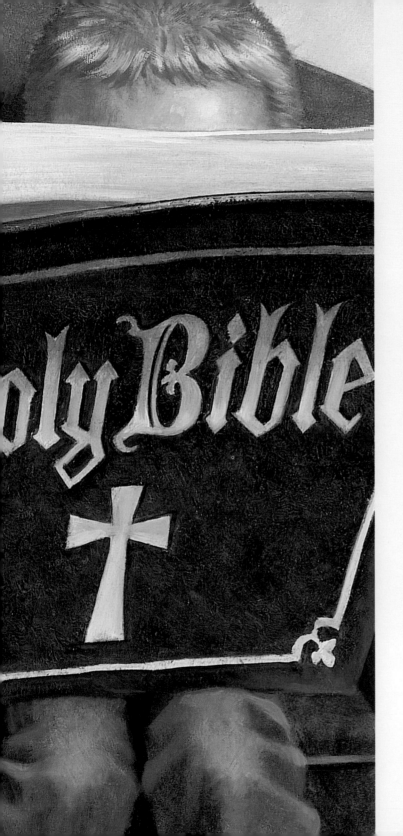

Why Doesn't God Talk to Me Out Loud?

Sometimes God does speak out loud to people. Do you remember the story about young Samuel?

"The boy Samuel … was lying down in the Lord's house. That's where the ark of God was kept … The Lord called out to Samuel. Samuel answered, 'Here I am.' He ran over to Eli. He said, 'Here I am. You called out to me.' But Eli said, 'I didn't call you. Go back and lie down.' So he went and lay down" (1 Samuel 3:1, 3–5).

This happened three times! Finally, Eli, the old blind priest, understood what was happening. He told Samuel to say, "Speak, I'm listening," if someone called out to him again. And sure enough God called out again and spoke to Samuel.

If God wanted to, he could even talk out loud to us, just like he talked to little Samuel. But sometimes God whispers things into our hearts to let us know what he wants us to do. And other times God speaks through the Bible.

God used to talk to his people through prophets. The prophets wrote down God's words, and those words were put into the Bible. Now when we want to hear God, all we have to do is open up our Bibles and read—or have someone read to us!

And if God never talks out loud to you—that's okay.

Why Did God Make People, Anyway?

Have you ever wondered why moms and dads who have no children adopt them? Is it just because they need company? Is it because their houses are so quiet that they want to hear giggles and squeals and bumps and bangs and little feet running up and down the stairs?

Maybe. But I think the main reason is that people who adopt little boys and girls are people who have extra love to give away. Do you suppose that's the way it was with God in the beginning? Maybe he said to himself: "I am full of love. I am love. I would like to give some of myself away."

So God made a man and a woman. He loved them and they loved him. He made them so that they could have children to love too. God knew that soon there would be giggles and squeals and bumps and bangs and little feet tearing up and down the pathways of his brand-new world. Remember … God is love. And he created a me and a you, so he could shower us with love. It was his good plan all along.

Then one sad day, the people God had made stopped loving him. But God went right on loving them. He had so much love that he gave his own precious Son to die for all of the people he had made—including you and me. Now he gives a forever home in heaven to all who ask Jesus to forgive them of their sins. I don't know about you, but it makes me want to love him back with all my heart!

Can I Hide from God?

I once had a friend named Steve who made a fort out of dirt and a big sheet of plywood. To get into his fort, he would slide the plywood back a little and slither inside. Then no one could see him. Steve really liked the idea that no one knew where he was—and he liked to brag about it too. Once he bragged to me that not even *God* could see him in his fort.

Well ... Steve was wrong. God said in the Bible: "Can anyone hide in secret places so that I can't see him? ... I fill heaven and earth." (Jeremiah 23:24).

God didn't have any problem at all seeing the little boy inside that muddy fort. God sees astronauts floating in their space shuttles. He sees sailors in submarines deep in the ocean. He sees explorers creeping into black caves. He can see us when it's light, and he can see us in the dark. He sees the good things people do and the bad things too.

Why would we want to hide from God, anyway—especially since he loves us so much? God sees us every minute of every day, and he loves us no matter what. He will help us, and if we are hiding because we have done wrong, he will forgive us.

Just How Much Does God Love Me?

Many truths about God are TOO BIG for our minds to hold. We can know a little about God's love, but we could never begin to stretch our thoughts around something so huge. Sometimes it helps me to think about God's love like this:

Imagine a thousand white-peaked mountains with their tops poking into space. Well, God's love is like a huge castle, soaring even higher than that! This castle of God's love is so huge it would take a lifetime just to walk around inside it and see all of its rooms and towers.

But do you know what? That castle of God's love can be all yours. God wants you to come to the castle and see how wonderful it is. He wants you to walk through its doorway and see, hear, and touch all of its wonders and delights—until you can't hold any more love in your heart.

God's love has no ending. We get to spend the rest of our lives here on earth and all of our lives in Heaven learning, seeing, and hearing about God's love.

Where Was Jesus before He Was Born?

We know that Jesus is God; just as God the Father is God. And we know that God has always been alive. That means that Jesus has always been alive too. So where was Jesus before he was born on earth?

We all like to think about that first Christmas night when Jesus came to our world as a newborn baby. But before he became a baby on earth, Jesus, God's Son, had lived in heaven with God the Father, God the Holy Spirit, and all the millions of shining, busy angels.

At the right time, Jesus turned his back on all the beauty and happiness of his forever home. And he stepped out of heaven and became a baby on earth.

It must have made the angels wide-eyed to see the King say good-bye and take those long steps—

—down

—down

—down

through black space to the little blue planet where you and I live.

But very soon angels came to earth too. Late on that same star-sprinkled night, those angels peeled back the sky just like you would tear open a sparkling Christmas present. They began to shout and sing the message that baby Jesus had been born.

The world had a Savior! The angel called it "Good News," and it *was* … it *is* … and it always *will* be!

What Does God Do All Day?

God is doing so many things all across his wide universe, I couldn't even begin to tell them all—even if I knew!

One thing he does is paint sunsets. Have you ever noticed how beautiful they are? God is a marvelous artist. He chooses just the colors he wants for his wonderful sunset paintings. Each sunset is different from the one before it. God chooses different colors and brushes to create his work. And while we're enjoying a beautiful sunset here, on the other side of the world, God is creating a brand-new sunrise for the boys and girls there.

Another thing God does is watch over you! Did you know he stays awake all the time, so he can?

"The Lord will keep you from every kind of harm.

He will watch over your life.

The Lord will watch over your life no matter where you go,

Both now and forever."

Psalm 121:7-8

What else does he do?

Jesus told a story about a boy who ran away from home and from his father. His father was so sad, and every day he watched for his son to come home. God is like that father. God waits and waits for us to turn around from going our own way to come home to him. When we do, his arms are wide open and there is a smile of welcome and joy on his face. God loves us so much! And he's never too busy for us!

Why Does God Let Bad Things Happen?

God is a good God. So why do bad things happen to people on earth—like getting sick?

When your throat hurts, your head aches, and your mom says you have a fever, it means you are sick. Some stubborn, invisible germ has attacked your body and you feel terrible.

Way back at the beginning of time, something terrible came into our world and it's been here ever since. It wasn't a germ or a virus. It was worse. It was sin, and it came into our world when Adam and Eve disobeyed God.

Then bad, sad things began to happen, and they still happen today. Whenever you see bad things happening, you know that the problem came into the world when Adam and Eve sinned. But there is a happy ending.

Jesus NEVER sinned. This meant that he was the only person who could take away all the sin and sickness of the whole world. The Bible says: "Christ didn't have any sin. But God made him become sin for us. So we can be made right with God because of what Christ has done for us" (2 Corinthians 5:21).

Those who receive the Lord Jesus as their Savior have their sins forgiven! They get to start life again with fresh, new hearts. And when they die, they get to live with God in his forever home!

Why Didn't Jesus Stay on Earth?

After Jesus came out of his grave alive again, he stayed with his friends for a while. Then he told them that he had to go back to heaven.

Before he left, Jesus promised to send his friends a new Friend. "The Father will send the Friend … the Holy Spirit … It is for your good that I am going away. Unless I go away, the Friend will not come to help you. But if I go, I will send him to you" (John 14:26; 16:6–7).

How could it be for our good for Jesus to go away? Why is it better to have the Friend—the Holy Spirit—with us?

It's like this. When Jesus was on earth in his human body, he could only be in one place at a time. But the Holy Spirit can be everywhere at once! He can be with me out on my mountain bike at the same time he's with you at a ball game. While we're still on this earth, the Holy Spirit is our special Friend, Helper, Partner, and Teacher.

Jesus said it would be best for him to go away. And if Jesus said it's best, then you can be sure that it is the very, very BEST!

When Will Jesus Come Back?

When Jesus comes back, we will all rise to meet him in the air. Just listen!

"The Lord himself will come down from heaven … We will be taken up in the clouds. We will meet the Lord in the air. And we will be with him forever" (1 Thessalonians 4:16–17).

Just think! There you are in school. Suddenly you hear the blast of a trumpet and a shout of joy. Before you can gasp, you will be high over the school, flying up, up, up toward the clouds And there will be Jesus, and he is just waiting to welcome you. The sky is full of excited angels and all your family and friends who love Jesus. Everyone is laughing and praising God as heaven's gate swings wide open to let us all in.

When will Jesus come back? We don't know. We are just supposed to keep watching for his coming. Jesus said, "No one knows… Not even the angels in heaven know. The Son does not know. Only the Father knows … So keep watch" (Matthew 24:36, 42).

I am looking for Jesus to come back for me. Let's pray for each other, and I'll look for you on top of a big white cloud. You'll know me. I'll be the one trying to do back flips.

How Can I Know for Sure that I'll Go to Heaven?

Are you sure you will be going to heaven when you leave this life? You don't have to worry because you *can* be sure. Jesus came to earth to make the way to heaven plain and clear.

He said: "Anyone who hears my word and believes him who sent me has eternal life. He will not be found guilty. He has crossed over from death to life" (John 5:24).

How do you give your life to Jesus? All you need to do is to say a prayer to him that goes something like this:

Dear Lord Jesus, thank you for inviting me to be your child and to someday live in your beautiful forever home. Thank you for dying on the cross for me. Please forgive all the bad, hurtful things I have done. I want to belong to you. I want you to be Lord and King of my life. Amen.

When you pray this prayer, you become a child of God who will someday go to heaven. So when you get to there, look for me. I'll be watching for you!